Da

Second series

The Dark Candle	978-184167-603-6
The Dark Machine	978-184167-601-2
The Dark Words	978-184167-602-9
Dying for the Dark	978-184167-604-3
Killer in the Dark	978-184167-605-0
The Day is Dark	978-184167-606-7
The Dark River	978-184167-745-3
The Bridge of Dark Tears	978-184167-746-0
The Past is Dark	978-184167-747-7
Playing the Dark Game	978-184167-748-4
The Dark Music	978-184167-749-1
The Dark Garden	978-184167-750-7

First series

The Dark Fire of Doom	978-184167-417-9
Destiny in the Dark	978-184167-422-3
The Dark Never Hides	978-184167-419-3
The Face in the Dark Mirror	978-184167-411-7
Fear in the Dark	978-184167-412-4
Escape from the Dark	978-184167-416-2
Danger in the Dark	978-184167-415-5
The Dark Dreams of Hell	978-184167-418-6
The Dark Side of Magic	978-184167-414-8
The Dark Glass	978-184167-421-6
The Dark Waters of Time	978-184167-413-1
The Shadow in the Dark	978-184167-420-9

Dark Man

The Dark Garden
by Peter Lancett
illustrated by Jan Pedroietta

Published by Ransom Publishing Ltd.
Radley House, 8 St. Cross Road, Winchester, Hampshire, UK
SO23 9HX
www.ransom.co.uk

ISBN   978 184167 750 7
First published in 2011

A CIP catalogue record of this book is available from the British Library.

Dark Man

The Dark Garden

by Peter Lancett

illustrated by Jan Pedroietta

Rans⬤m

Chapter One:
Time to Die

The world seems upside down.

The Dark Man has been captured, but he remains calm.

A rope is tied around his ankle.

He hangs by this rope, suspended from the branch of an ancient tree.

The tree stands in the middle of a lawn in a tidy garden, bathed by silver moonlight.

There is a leather collar around his neck, with silver handcuffs attached to the back, tight around his wrists.

The garden belongs to a house, far from the city.

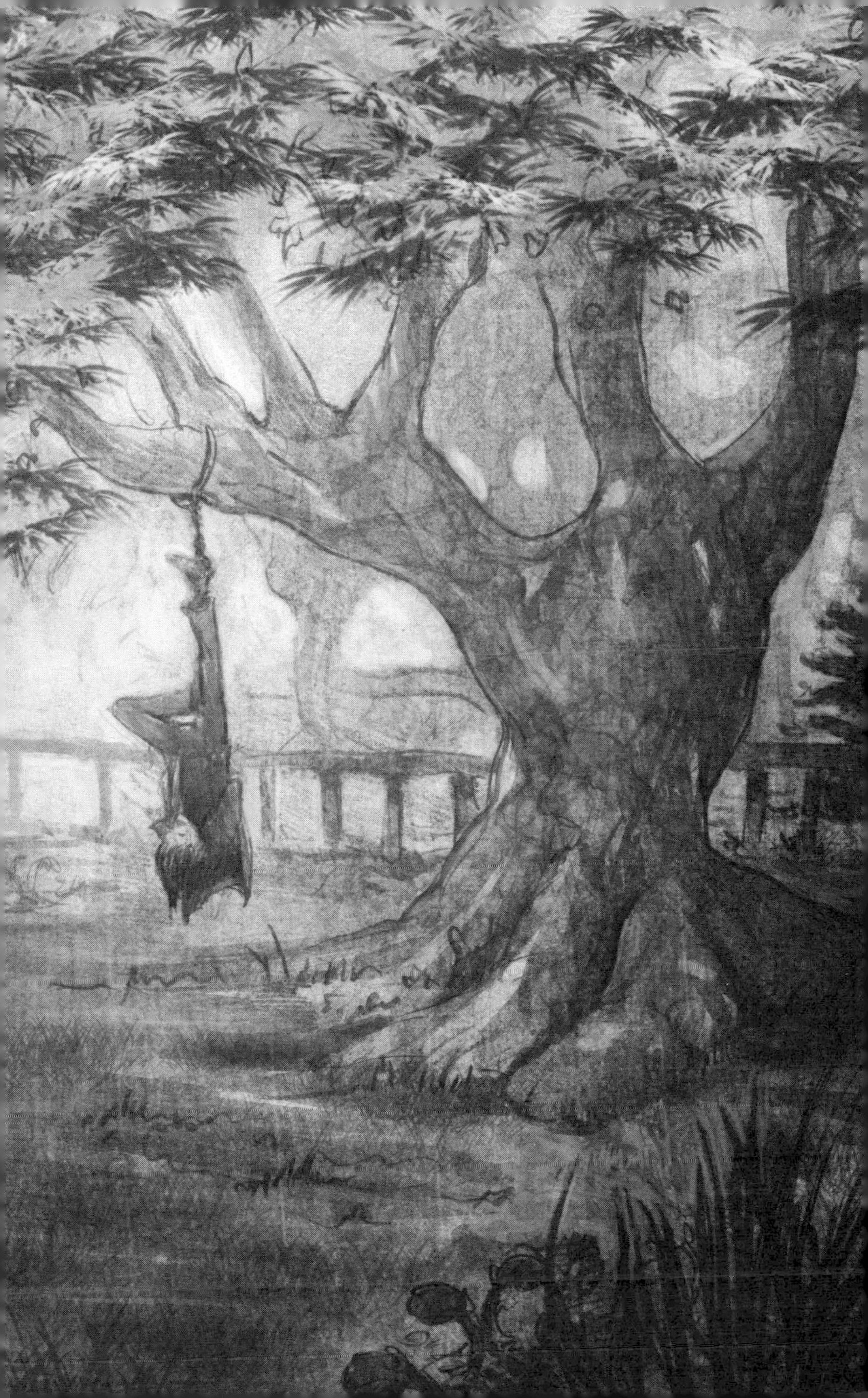

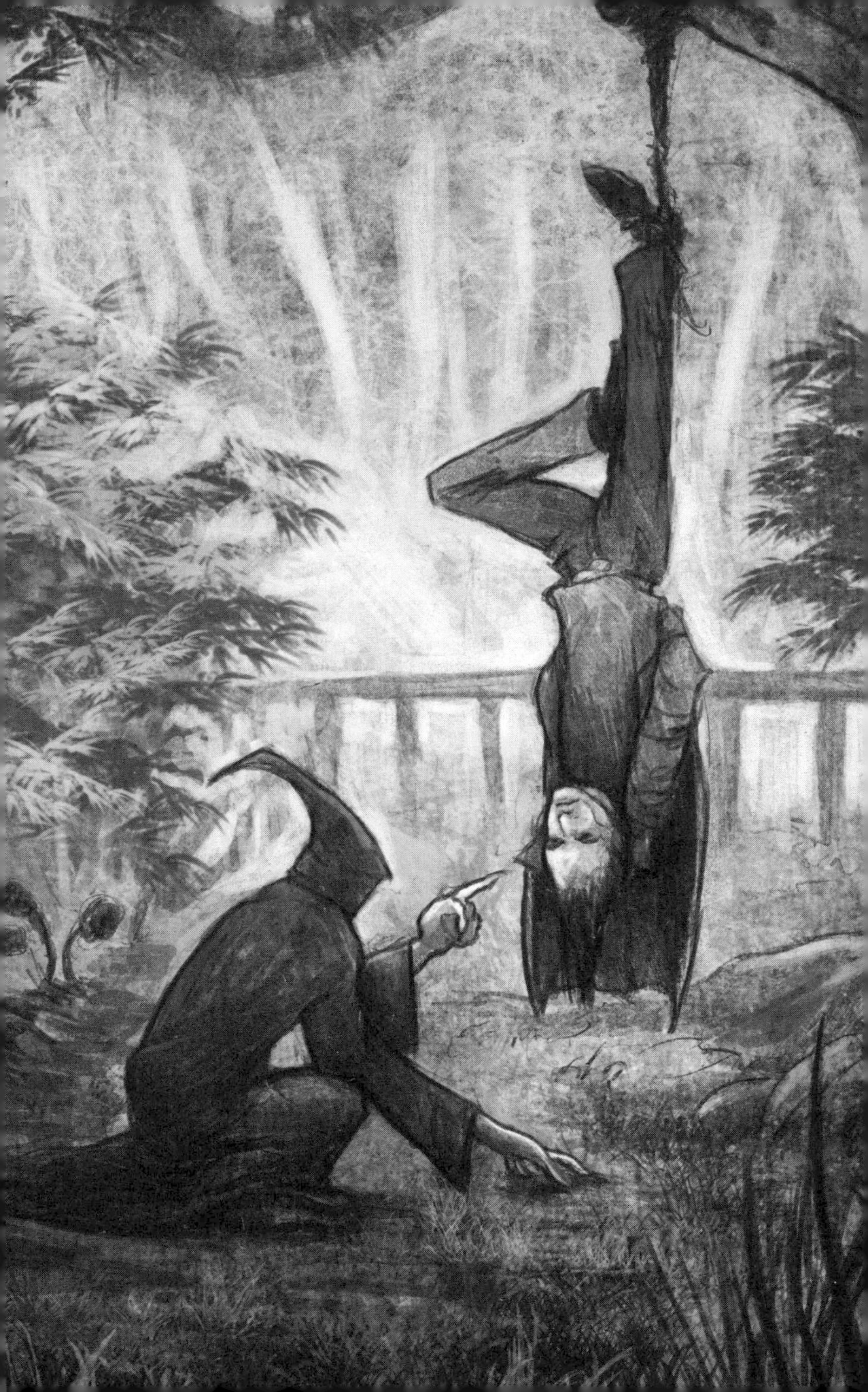

A dark figure comes to stand before him.

Slowly, the figure lowers itself to sit on the grass.

It is a Shadow Master.

'Why have you come here?' the Shadow Master asks.

'To put a stop to your plans,' the Dark Man answers.

The Shadow Master shakes his head. 'We are too strong and too many,' he says.

The Dark Man does not reply.

After a minute, the Shadow Master speaks again.

'We have been watching you,' he says.

'You have the power to work in the day and the night. Why do you oppose us?'

'Because people deserve to live in freedom,' the Dark Man says. 'You want to make slaves of them.'

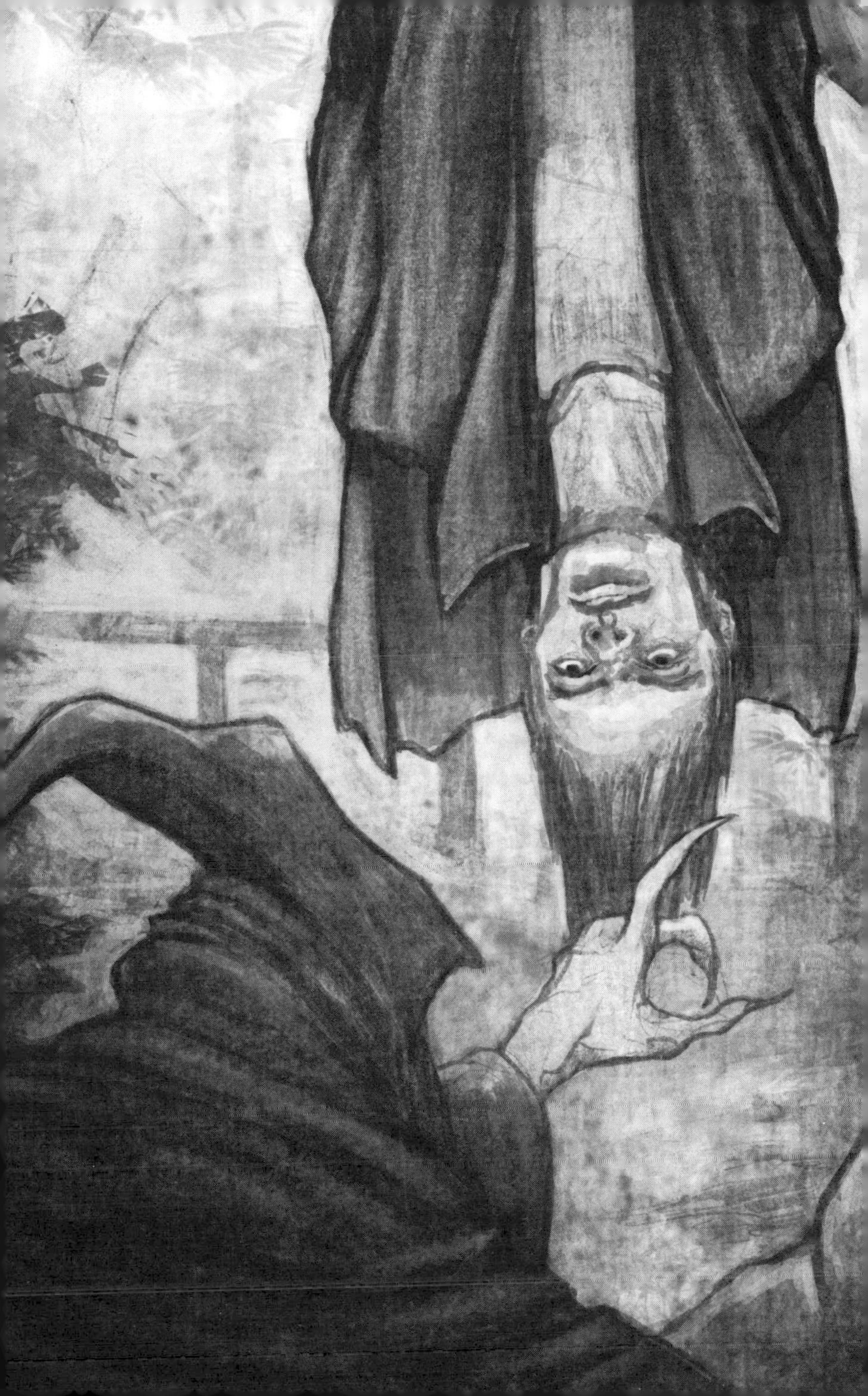

The Shadow Master laughs.

'You say that they will be slaves. We say that we will bring order to their lives. How can that be wrong?'

The Dark Man does not answer.

'You should join us,' the Shadow Master says. 'With us, you could rule the world.'

'Never!' the Dark Man says.

The Shadow Master rises. 'Then you must die. We will come to drain you of your power before the Sun rises.'

Chapter Two:
The Flowers Smile

The Dark Man watches as the Shadow Master walks away.

He looks at the garden.

He sees that the flowers have closed, waiting for the morning sunshine to waken them.

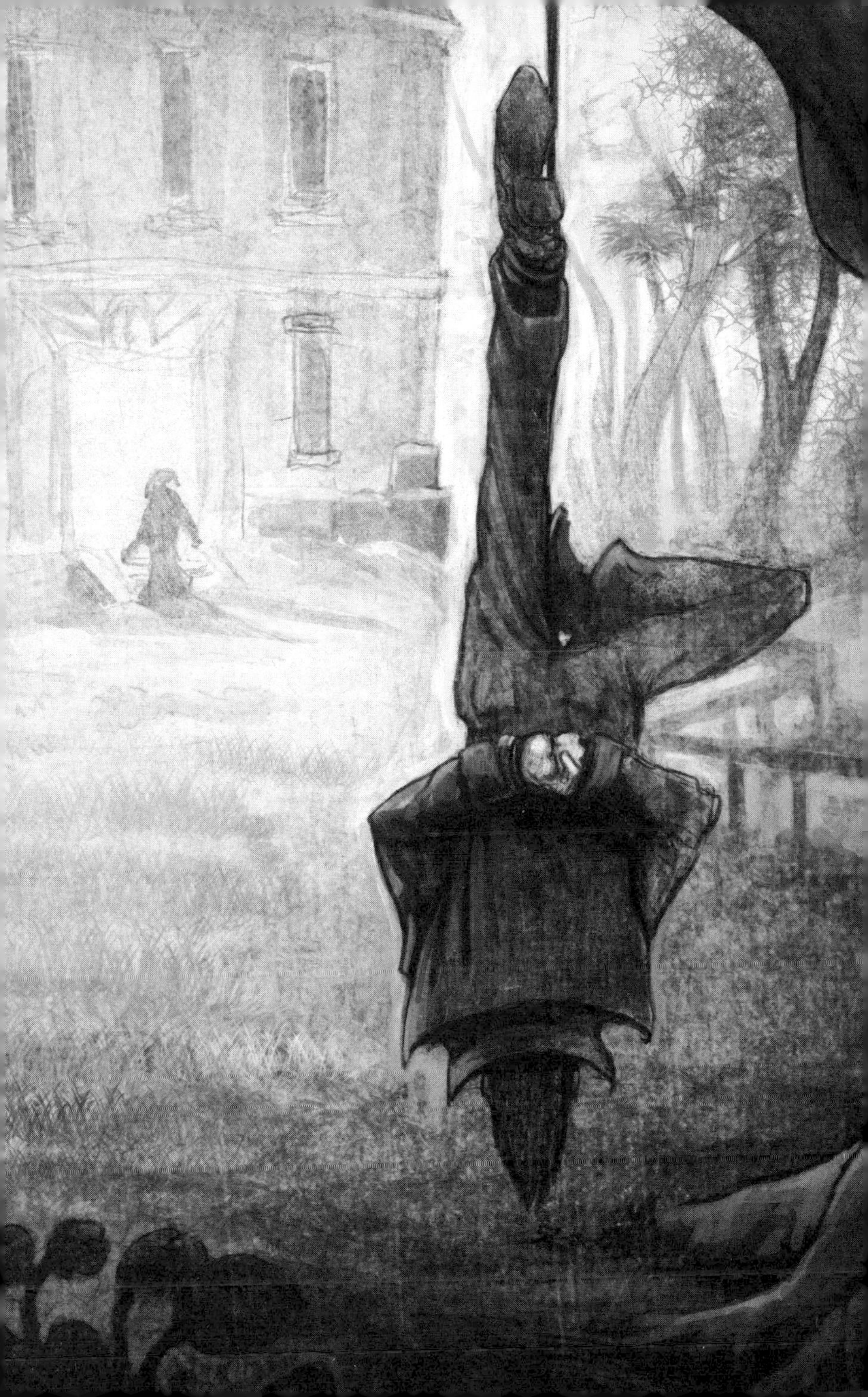

He twists his hands, trying to slip free of the silver handcuffs.

But the Shadow Masters have used magic to make them strong, and they close tighter against his wrists.

Suddenly he sees a slight movement, behind a bush on the far side of the garden.

A large creature scuttles through the shadows, moving from shrub to shrub.

Then he notices something magical.

Whenever the creature stops, the moonlight shining on the flowers nearby seems brighter.

The flowers begin to unfold, as though they are mistaking moonlight for sunlight.

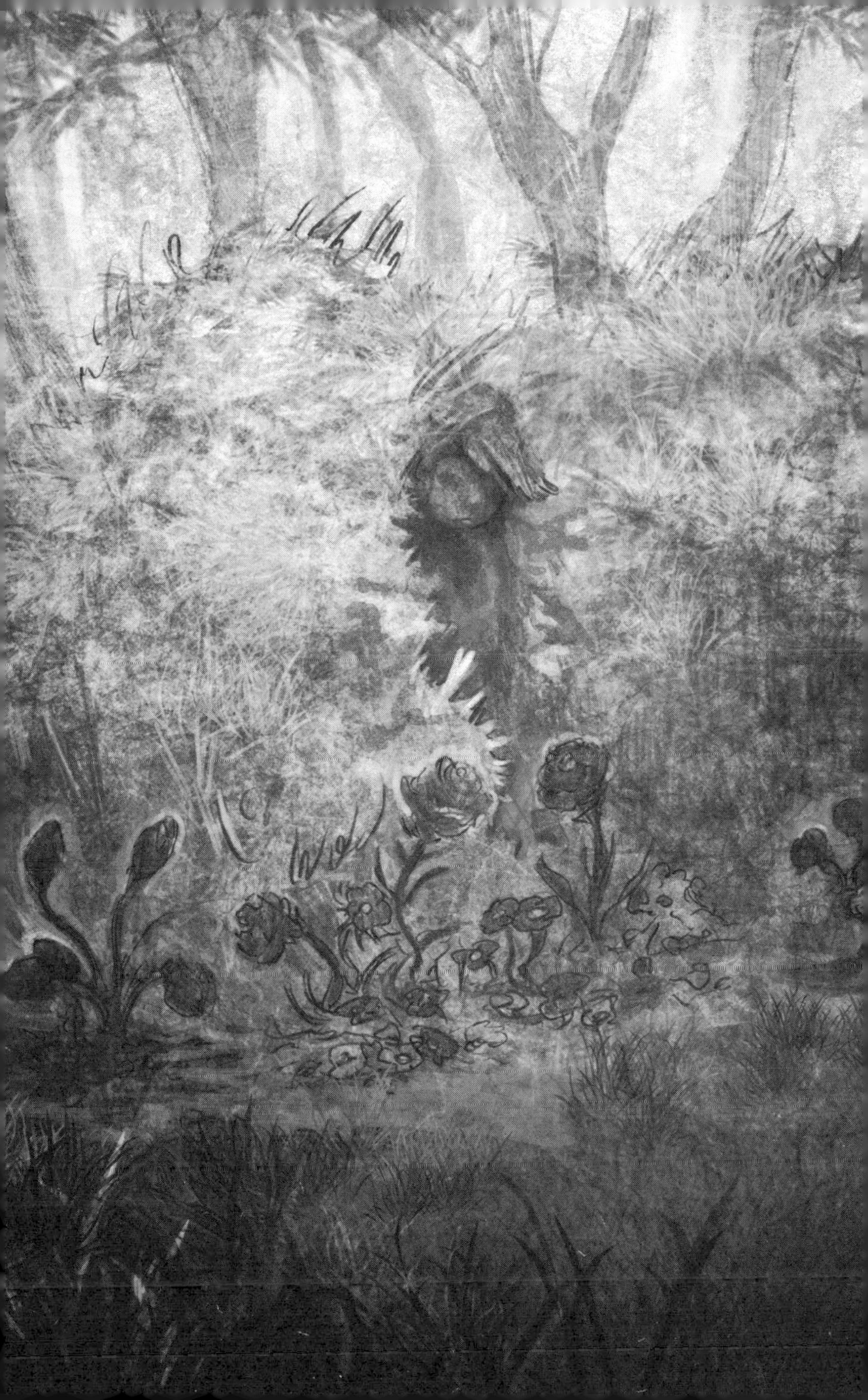

Then the creature is crawling across the lawn towards him.

And the Dark Man sees that it is a little girl.

When she reaches him, she stands upright.

'Hello,' she says. 'I am Claire. This is my garden.'

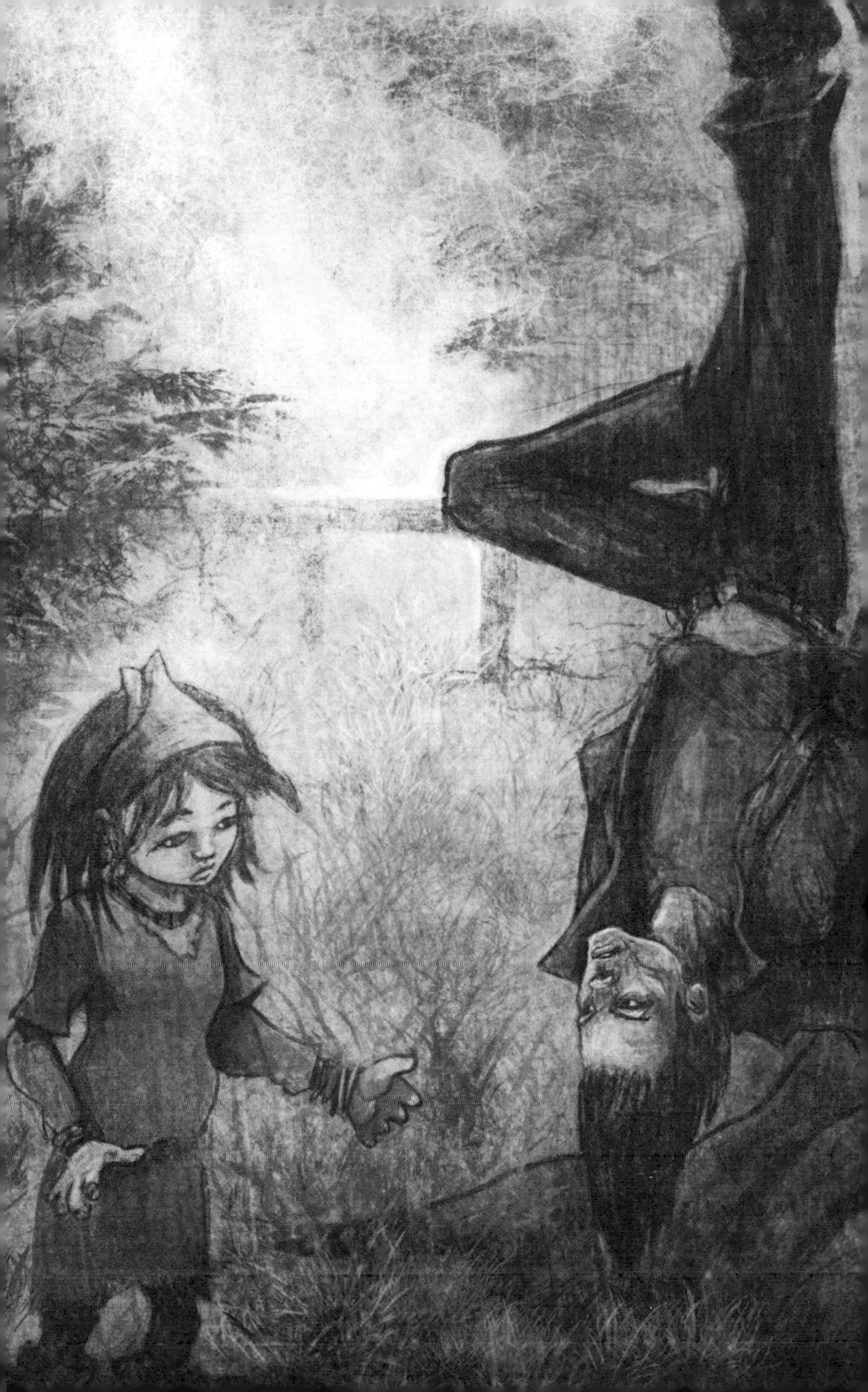

'You seem to draw power from the moonlight,' the Dark Man says.

'Moonlight is silver and cold,' Claire replies.

'I can make moonlight warm, so that the flowers smile in the darkness.'

'Don't the flowers smile enough in the sunlight?' the Dark Man asks.

Claire frowns. 'I cannot see them in the sunlight. It is too bright and it hurts me.'

'That is sad,' the Dark Man says.

'Why are you hanging here like this?' Claire asks. 'Did the bad men put you here?'

She is walking around behind him, so that the Dark Man can no longer see her.

'Yes,' the Dark Man answers. 'They are called Shadow Masters.'

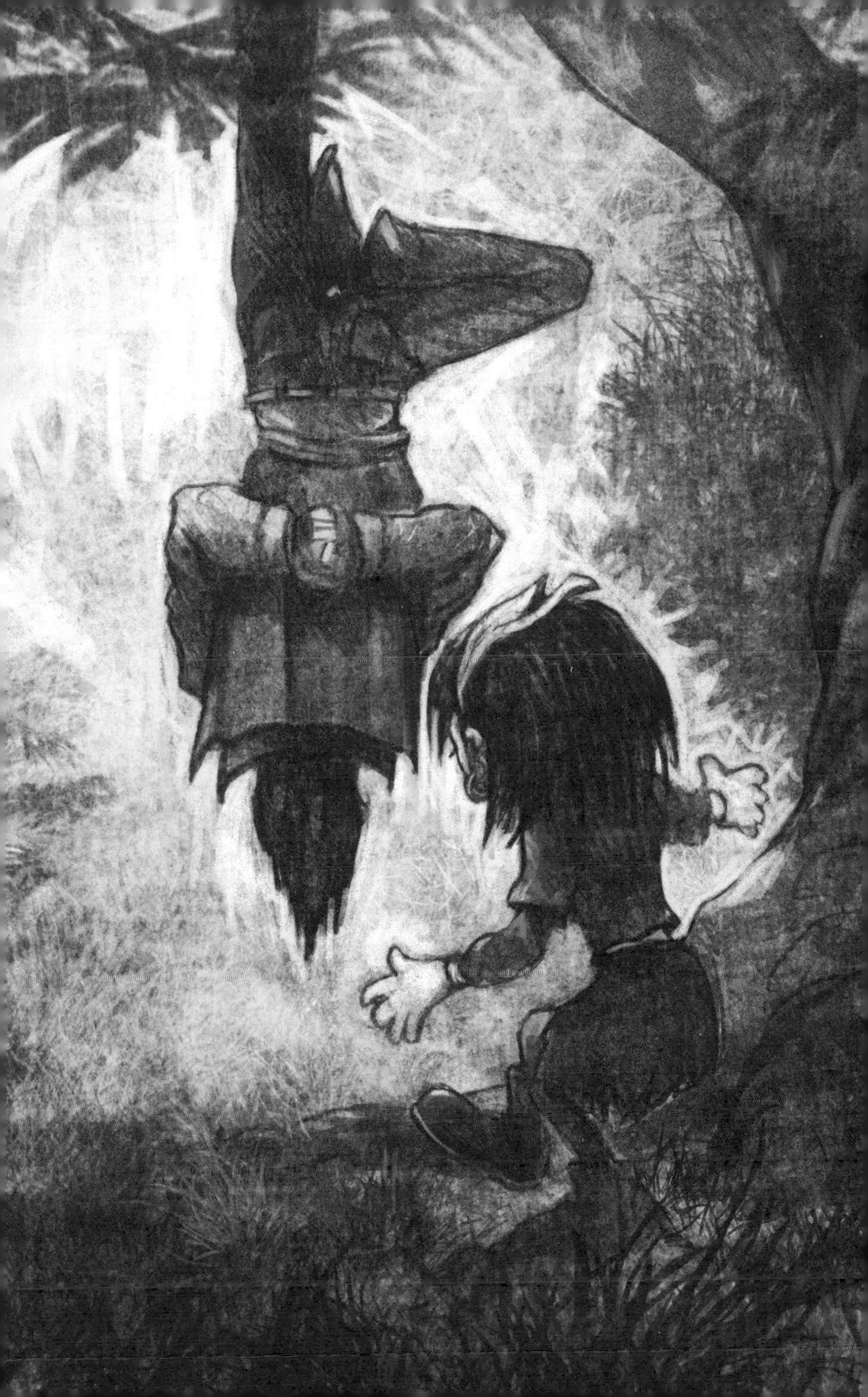

Chapter Three:
Weak Magic

Claire inspects the handcuffs binding the Dark Man's wrists.

'Don't those handcuffs hurt?' she asks.

'Yes,' the Dark Man tells her. 'But I cannot get free.'

'They are made of silver,' Claire says. 'I can do things with silver. Would you like me to set you free?'

The Dark Man shakes his head.

'The Shadow Masters have used magic on this silver. And they will be coming back soon.'

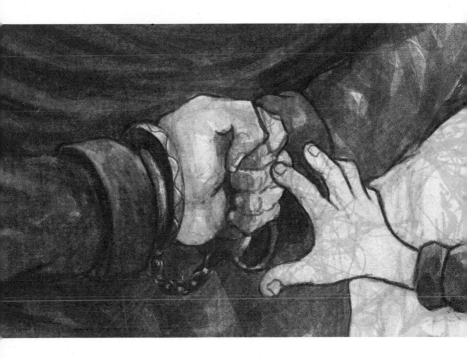

Claire giggles.

'Their magic is weak,' she says, placing her small hands upon the silver handcuffs.

The Dark Man feels the silver getting warm.

'Are you a Master of Silver?' the Dark Man asks.

Claire does not reply.

The Dark Man feels that the handcuffs are no longer cutting into his skin.

The silver is getting hot, and it is expanding.

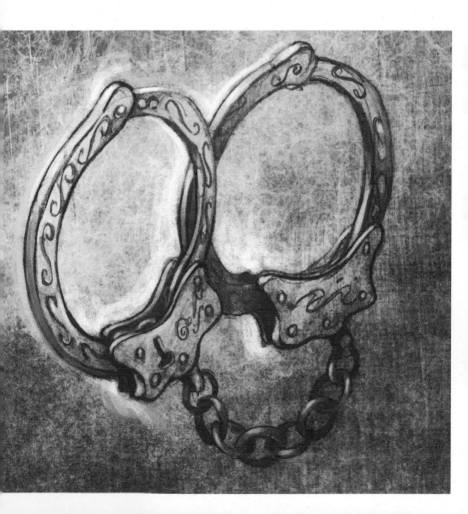

Then the Dark Man notices something moving, beyond the lawn.

Two black figures seem to rise from the shadows near the house.

They are Shadow Masters.

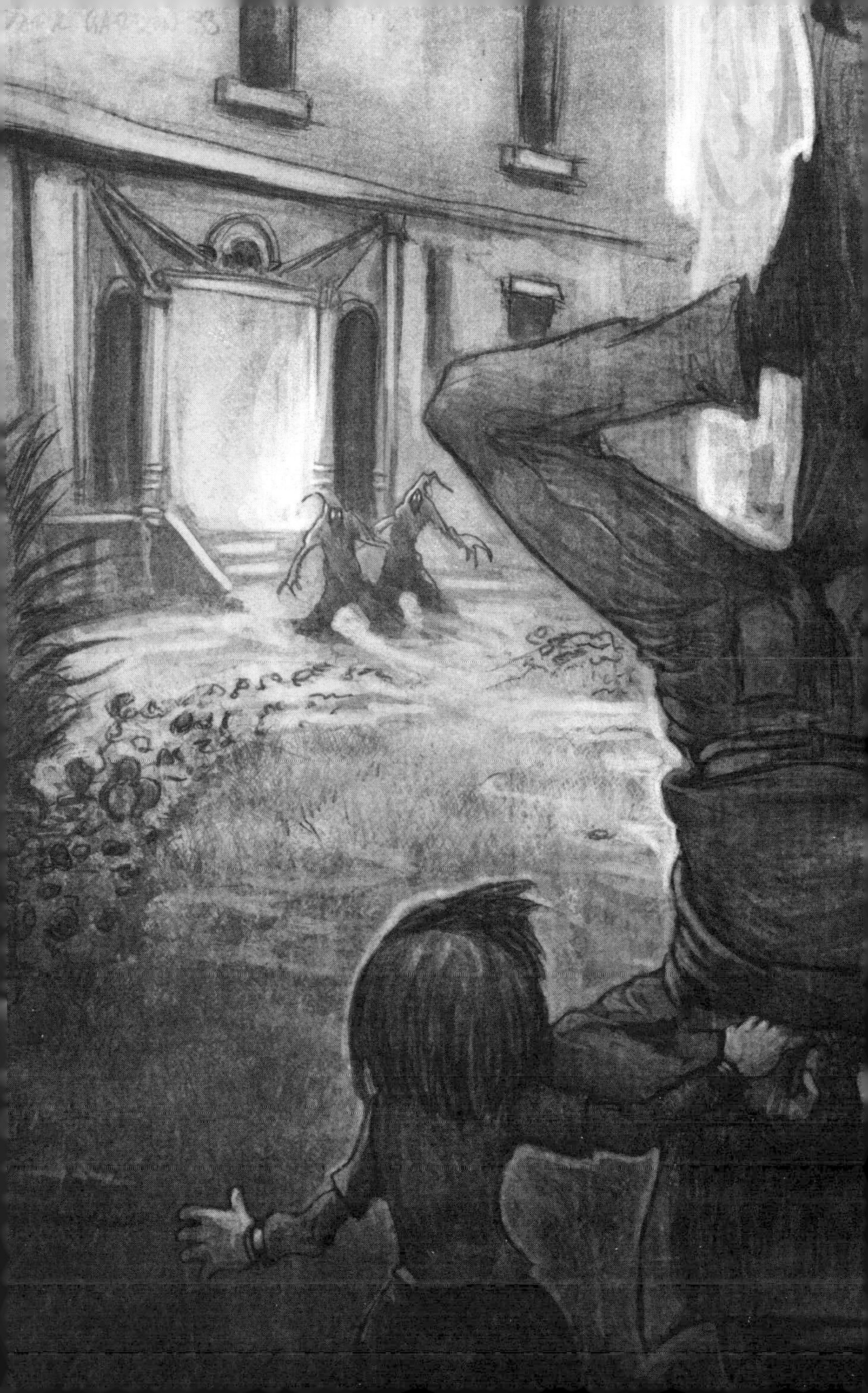

The Shadow Masters are walking towards the lawn.

The Dark Man can see them clearly in the moonlight.

'You must hide,' he says to Claire. 'Two Shadow Masters are coming this way.'

'I have seen them,' Claire says. 'They do not frighten me.'

She moves to stand beside him.

Chapter Four:
Silver and Gold

The Shadow Masters have almost reached the flower border.

Claire seems to glow with silver light, as though she is drawing all the moonlight into her body.

The silver glow spreads from her feet, across the lawn, out to the flower border.

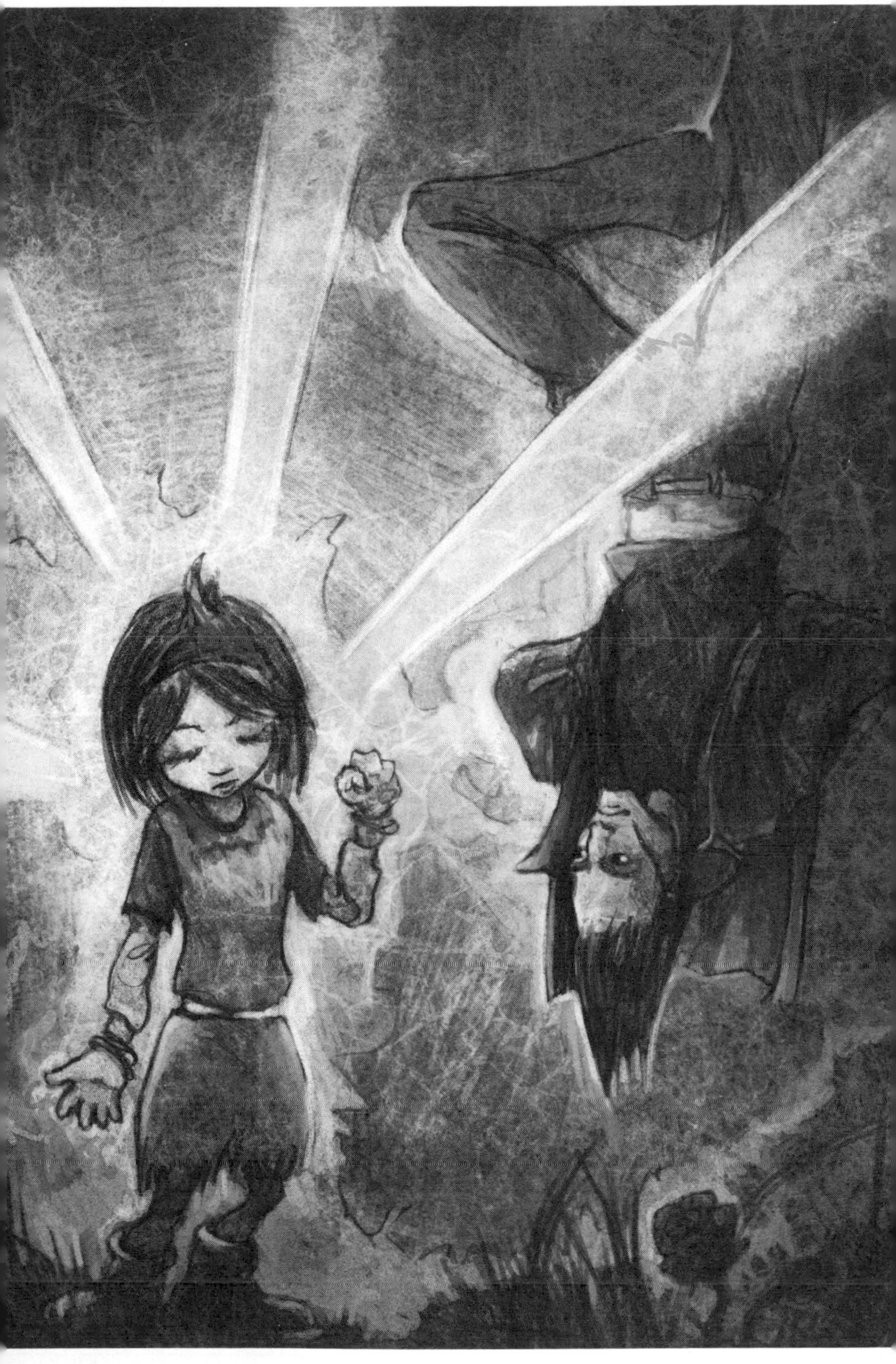

All at once, the flowers burst into life, and all their petals open.

A silver curtain of light rises up from the flower bed, lighting up the Shadow Masters.

The Shadow Masters scream.

The light is hurting them.

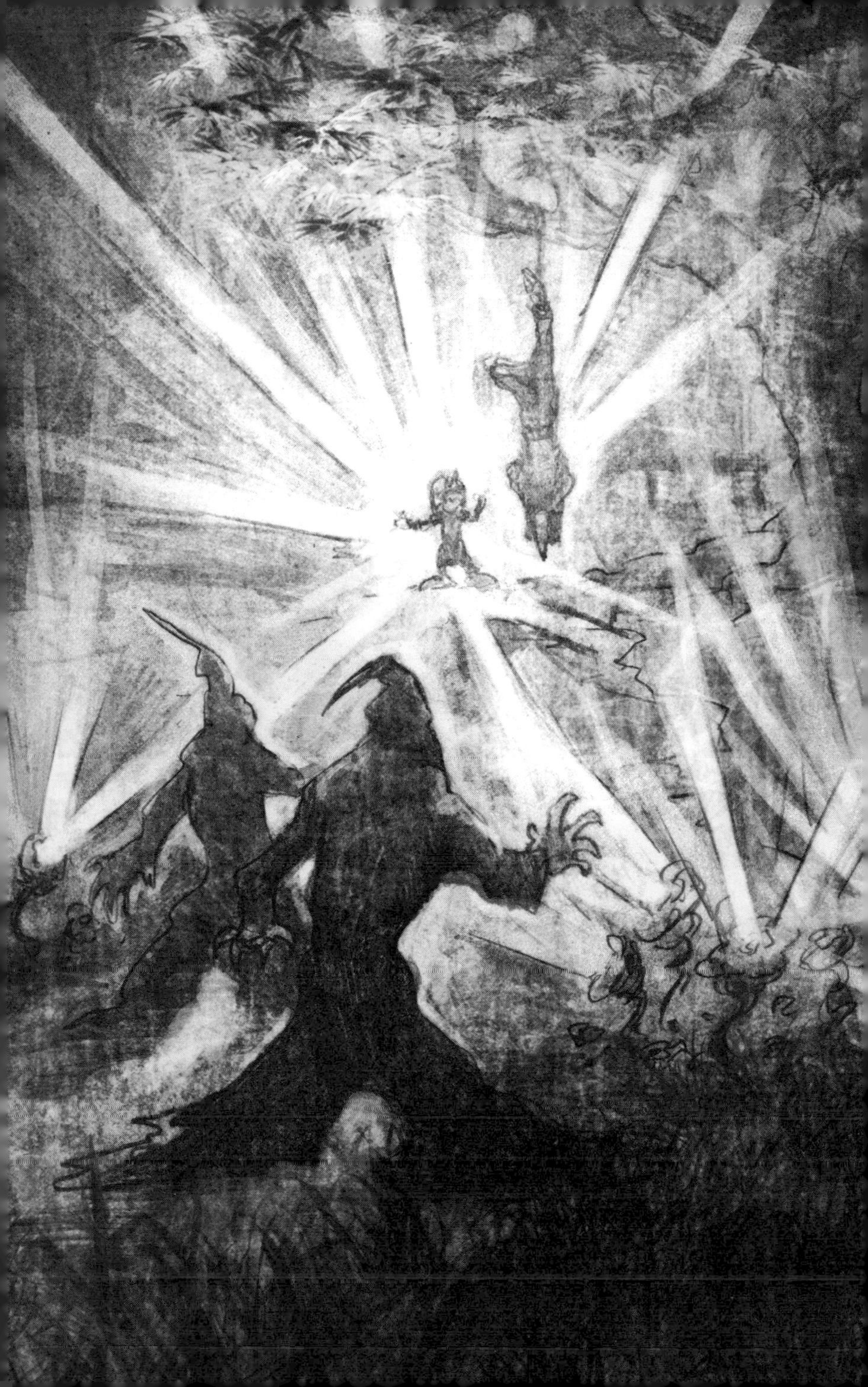

Then the silver light becomes golden, just like sunlight.

The Shadow Masters struggle, but their cloaks begin to burn.

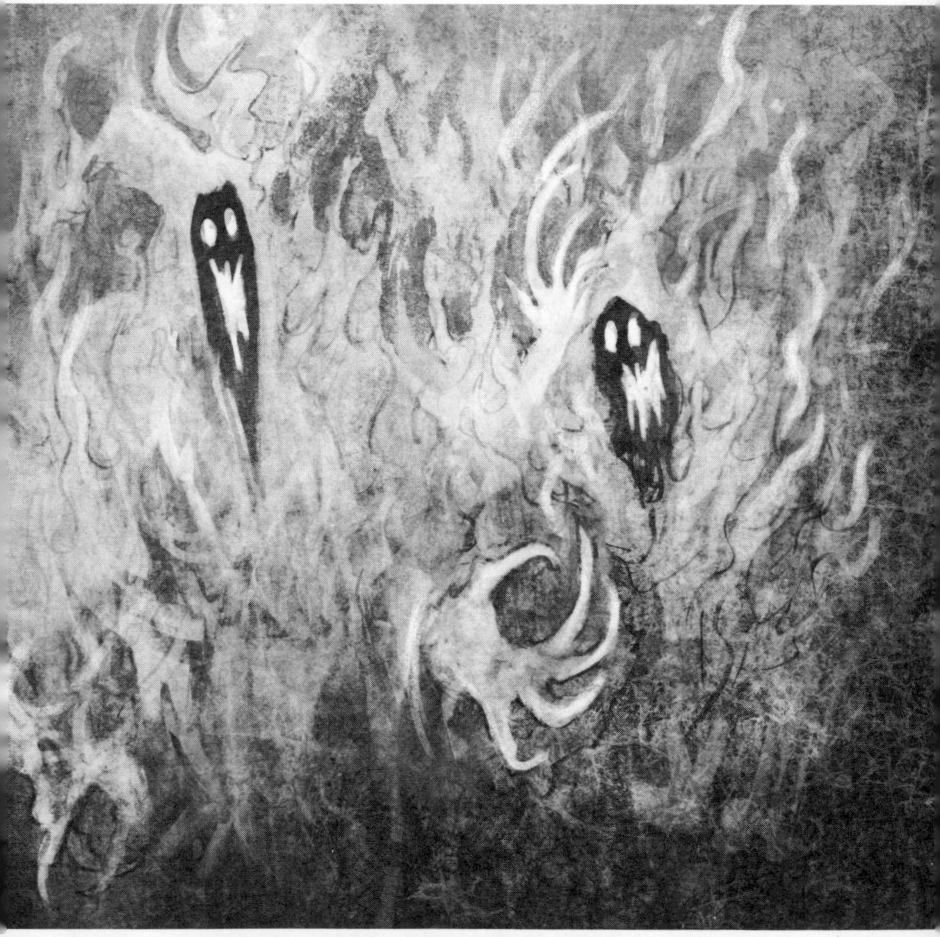

As flames consume the Shadow Masters and burn them to ash, the Dark Man notices Claire.

The light surrounding her is golden.

But Claire looks tired and weak.

As the golden light fades, Claire melts into shining liquid.

Soon, she is just a golden puddle on the grass.

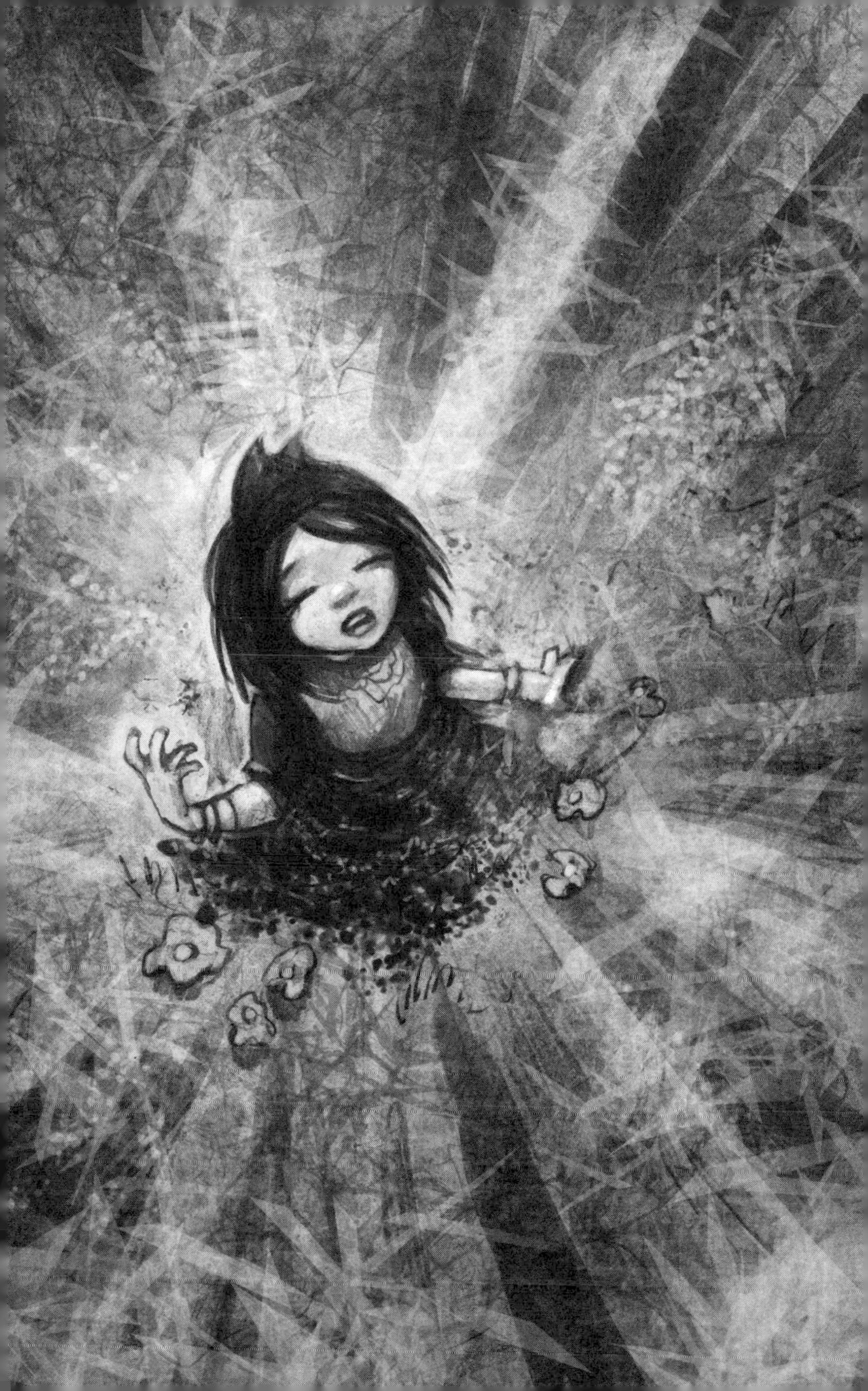

Behind his neck, the Dark Man feels the handcuffs break into small pieces and fall to the ground.

He frees himself from the rope and looks at them.

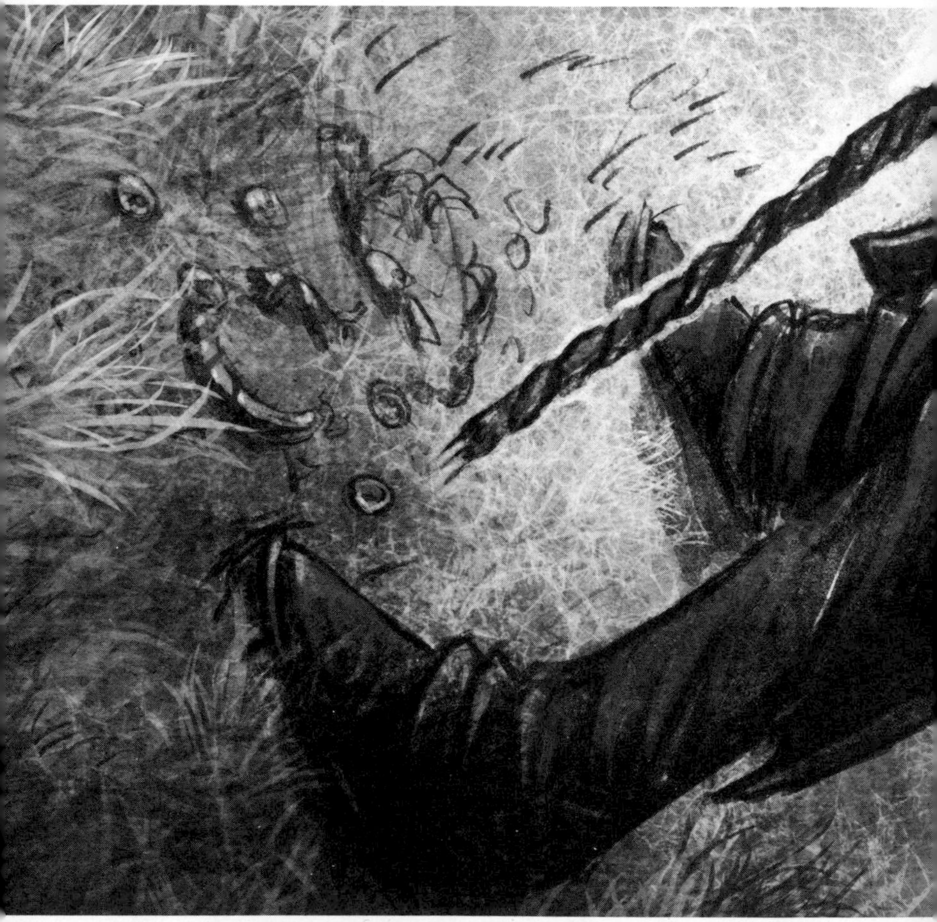

The pieces of silver have become gold.

He had been wrong about Claire.

She was not a Master of Silver.

She was a Master of Gold.

Her magic came from the light of the Sun, not the Moon.

He remembers that moonlight is really sunlight, reflected by the Moon.

He wonders what has happened to Claire.

He would like to thank her and learn more of her secrets.

In any event, he will come back to this house.

There is still work to be done here.

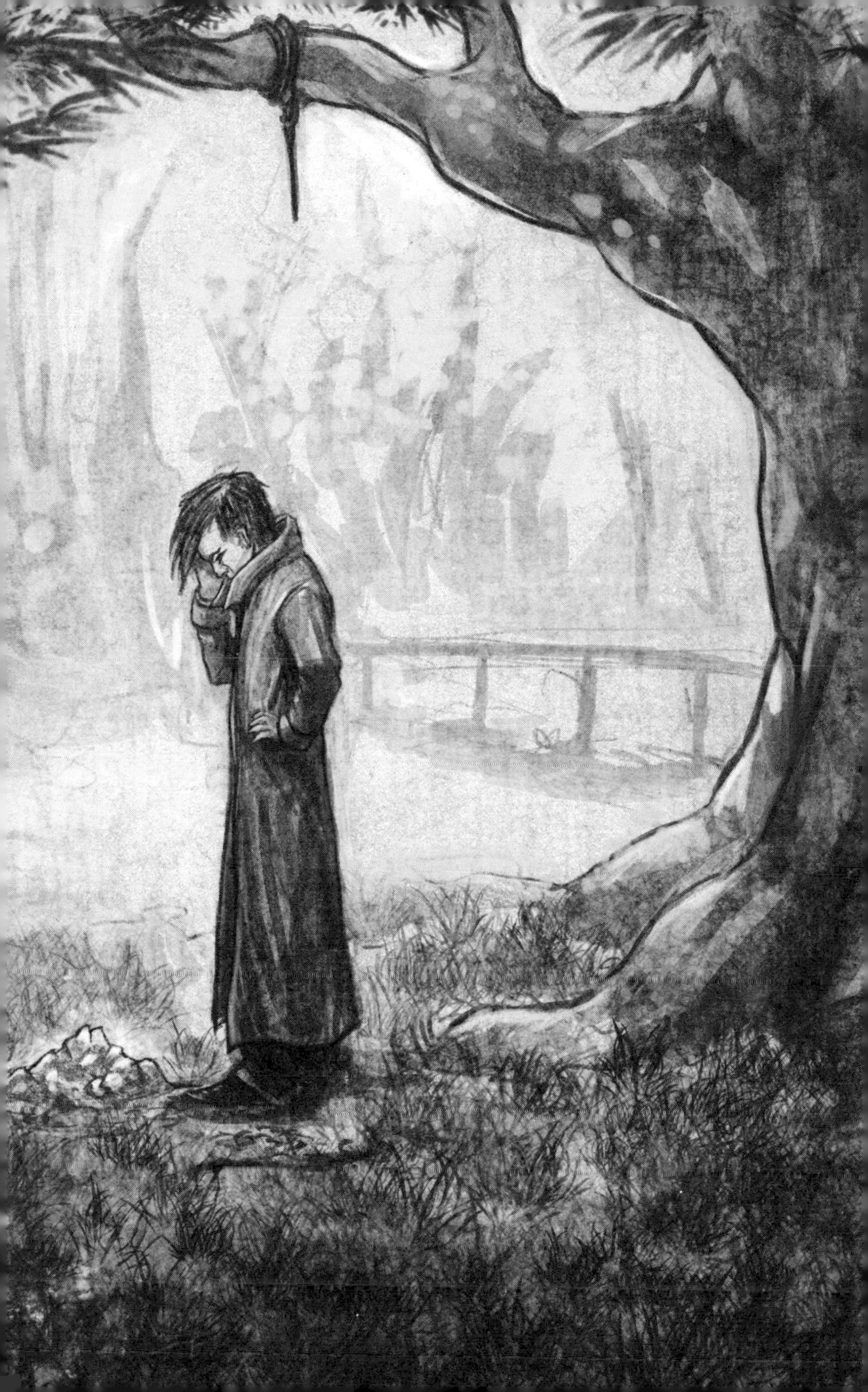

The author

Peter Lancett is a writer, editor and film maker.
He has written many books, and has just made
a feature film, *The Xlitherman*.

Peter now lives in New Zealand and California.